The Naughtiest Fairy's
Naughty New Friend

Written and
Illustrated by

Nick Ward

Albury Children's

The Naughtiest Ever Fairy sat at her kitchen table and sulked.

"I want someone to play with," she said.
"Someone naughty and fun - **just like me!**"

And then she had an idea...

If she wanted a friend, she could make one!
(She was a fairy, after all.)
"Brilliant!" she cried, flicking through
her book of spells.
"Here we are."

"Two frogs, one snail,
some stinky garlic,
And a lizards tail."

she sang, mixing the
ingredients into a bowl.

"Salt for fun,
and a pinch of pepper
for naughtiness..."

Extra
Sneezy
Pepper

Eyes!

"**Whoops!**" she cried, as she knocked the whole bag of pepper into her bowl. "Oh never mind." She waved her magic wand over the mixture.

"Fantastic!" cheered the new naughty fairy.
"Let's have some fun!"

The two friends went straight to the giant's castle. The giant was stomping about in his heavy gardening boots, watering his flowers.

"He's much too noisy," said the naughty fairy. "Watch this."

She waved her magic wand, and...

Kazim!

The giant started to inflate
like a huge balloon.
"What's happening?" he cried
as he floated, light as a feather, across the valley.
"**Get me down!**"
"Hee, hee," laughed the fairies and away they flew.

"I can be much naughtier than that," said the new naughty fairy as they flew past the village school.

The two fairies peered through the window where old Miss Munchet was reading to her class.

" AND THE MOST FEARSOME DINOSAUR OF ALL," SHE SAID, "WAS... "

(The new naughty fairy waved her wand.)

"That was brilliant," laughed the new naughty fairy when they got home. "I'm the naughtiest fairy ever."

"No, you're the **silliest fairy ever!**"

"Then I'll make a new friend," said the new naughty fairy, grabbing the naughty fairy's bowl of magic mix.

"No, I'm the naughtiest fairy ever," said the naughty fairy.

"Oh yeah?" said the naughty fairy, stamping her foot, "I'm not playing with you anymore."

She rushed outside. "Watch this," she cried, waving her magic wand...

POP!
There was another
naughty fairy.

And **that** naughty fairy said,
"I want a new friend."

POP... and that naughty fairy made a new friend, POP, until...

POP! POP! POP!

"This," said the naughty fairy, "is the result of too much pepper. STOP!"

But the fairies kept on appearing;
and each new fairy was being **very, very** naughty.

They made the grass turn blue and the sky green;
hills wobbled like jelly and the clouds rained ink;
rats as big as cats chased dogs that hopped like frogs!
Soon, everything was in a terrible muddle!

POP!

Ping!

"**Stop!**" yelled the naughty fairy.
(Enough, after all, is enough!)
But each time she made one fairy disappear,
a new fairy materialized.

"**How on earth am I going
to stop them?**" she cried, when...

"Watch out below!" called the giant, falling from the sky as the spell wore off.

CRASH! The giant landed in a cloud of pink, peppery, magic dust.

Kazam!

All the naughty fairies disappeared...

...all except the naughtiest ever fairy.
"Well done, Giant," she gasped.
"You're a hero."
"Oh, it was nothing,"
sneezed the giant through
a fog of pepper dust.

"Atchoo!"

"Now I think I can
take a well
earned rest,"
sighed the
naughty fairy,
making her
way indoors.

For Linda Blundell

who had a great idea.
N.W.

Way too many giants!

Published by Albury Books in 2016
Albury Court, Albury, Thame, OX9 2LP, United Kingdom

Sales and Enquiries:
Kuperard Publishers and Distributors
59 Hutton Grove, London, N12 8DS
Tel: +44 (0) 208 446 2440 | Fax: +44 (0) 208 446 2441
sales@kuperard.co.uk | www.kuperard.co.uk

Text © Nick Ward · Illustrations © Nick Ward
The rights of Nick Ward to be identified as the author and illustrator have been
asserted by them in accordance with the Copyright, Designs and Patents Act, 1988

ISBN 978-1-910571-50-7 (paperback)

A CIP catalogue record for this book is available from the British Library
10 9 8 7 6 5 4 3
Printed in the United Kingdom